To Lily, Emma, and Ben Helfrich

— M. A. H.

For the Goats, Arthur and Nancy

— N. B. W.

First Edition

Library of Congress Cataloging-in-Publication Data
Hoberman, Mary Ann.
    Bill Grogan's goat / adapted by Mary Ann Hoberman ; illustrated by Nadine Bernard
Westcott. — 1st ed.
        p. cm.
    Summary: Presents the familiar rhyme about a pesky goat that gets in trouble for eating
shirts off the clothesline.
    ISBN 0-316-36232-8
    1. Children's songs — Texts. [1. Goats — Songs and music. 2. Songs.] I. Westcott, Nadine
Bernard, ill. II. Title.

PZ8.3.H66 Bi 2002
782.42—dc21
[E]

00-050008

10 9 8 7 6 5 4 3 2 1

TWP

Printed in Singapore

The illustrations for this book were done in watercolor and ink.
The text was set in Triplex, and the display type is handlettered.

BILL GROGAN'S GOAT

adapted by
Mary Ann Hoberman
illustrated by
Nadine Bernard Westcott

 Megan Tingley Books

Little, Brown and Company
Boston New York London

Bill Grogan's goat
Was feeling fine.

Ate three red shirts
Right off the line.

Bill grabbed the goat
By the wool of his back

And tied him to
The railroad track.

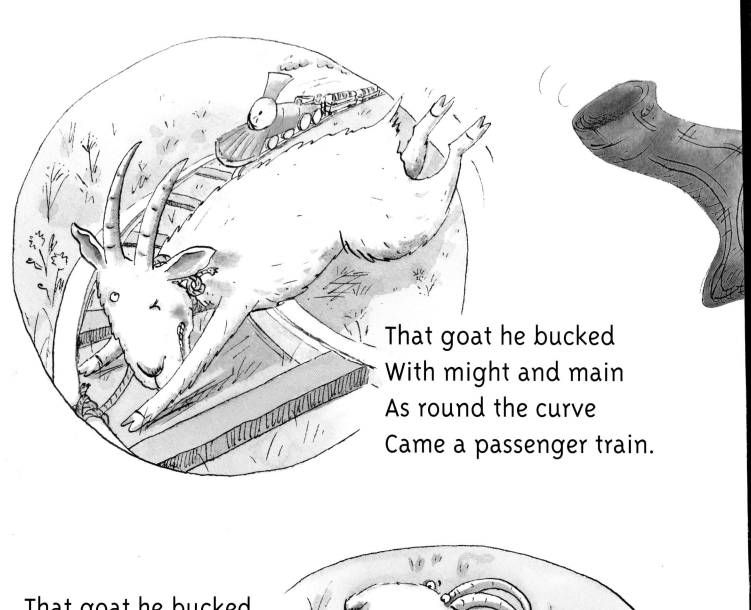

That goat he bucked
With might and main
As round the curve
Came a passenger train.

That goat he bucked
With might and main,
Coughed up those shirts

And flagged the train.

The engineer stopped
When he saw red.
"Why, it's a goat!"
He loudly said.

He took his knife
And cut the cord

And asked the goat
To come on board.

Bill Grogan's goat
Took a great jump

And landed on
A fluffy lump.

A sheep sprang up
And shouted, "Ouch!
I guess you thought
I was a couch!"

The goat cried, "Sheep,
Have you been hurt?
Forgive me, please,
And take a shirt."

The sheep went, "Baah!
That's very kind.
I'll put it on
If you don't mind."

The goat sat down
Upon a chair.

The chair stood up.
Oh, what a scare!

The chair turned out
To be a pig.
It was quite fat
And also big.

Bill Grogan's goat
Felt very sad.
Gave pig a shirt,
Said, "Don't be mad."

The pig went, "Oink!
That's really neat!
A new red shirt
Is quite a treat!"

Bill Grogan's goat
Felt rather sore.
He saw a rug
Upon the floor.

The rug jumped up!
The rug yelled, "Ow!"
It was no rug.
It was a cow!

Bill Grogan's goat
Got on his knees.
"Cow, take this shirt.
Forgive me, please."

"Please take this shirt,
The last I've got."
The cow said, "Moo!
And thanks a lot!"

The engineer said,
"It's time to eat.
I'd like you all
To take a seat."

The others were
So impolite,
Bill Grogan's goat
Got not a bite.

The dinners landed
On their shirts,
From macaroni
To desserts!

The engineer said,
"I've never seen
Such dirty shirts!
Go wash them clean!"

The hungry goat
Was sitting by.
He saw the shirts
Hung up to dry.

They looked so fresh.
They looked so fine.

He ate all three
Right off the line.